Christine Thorburn

Spooky

A ghost play

Ernst Klett Sprachen
Stuttgart

1. Auflage   1 $^{12\ 11\ 10\ 9}$ | 2010 09 08 07

Alle Drucke dieser Auflage können im Unterricht nebeneinander
benutzt werden, sie sind untereinander unverändert. Die letzte Zahl
bezeichnet das Jahr dieses Druckes.

© Ernst Klett Sprachen GmbH, Stuttgart 1993.
Alle Rechte vorbehalten.
Internetadresse: http://www.klett.de

Umschlag: Christian Gutendorf
Satz: Steffen Hahn, Kornwestheim
Druck: typopress, Leinfelden
Printed in Germany.

ISBN 978-3-12-545420-0

Contents

Foreword 5

List of characters 6

Scene One: Arrival 7

Scene Two: The Pudding 11

Scene Three: The Highlander 17

Scene Four: The Flag 23

Scene Five: The Writing on the Wall 28

Scene Six: Costumes 34

Scene Seven: The Lady 41

Teacher's Notes 47

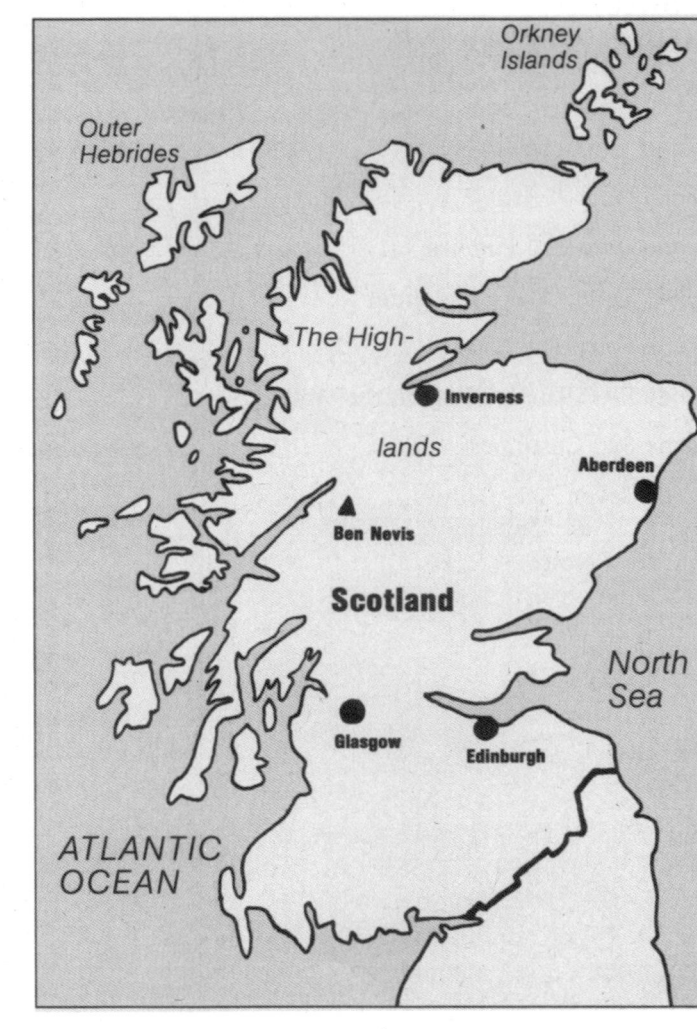

Foreword

Dear pupils,

Please do not just read this play. Act it! You'll have much more fun that way and you'll be speaking real English, too. What about doing it for other classes? Or for your parents and friends at a school fête? You could also record it, or even film it.

    Whatever you do, I hope you enjoy yourselves.

                Yours sincerely,
                Christine Thorburn.

Characters

Class 2A:
Jamie
Morag [ˈmɔːræg]
Katy
Alistair [ˈælɪstər]
David
Paula
Murdo
Anne
Mr Henderson, teacher

Class 2B:
Willie
Alison
Joan
Heather [ˈheðə]
Lorna
Michael
Robert
Tom
Mrs Robertson, teacher

Mr Grant, the warden

Second-year pupils from a school in Edinburgh are spending a week of their Easter holidays at an outdoor centre in the Highlands.

Scene One: Arrival.

(The boys of class 2A come into the common room with their rucksacks.)

Jamie:	Gosh, this place is ancient.
Alistair:	What did you expect? It was built in the seventeenth century.
Jamie:	I thought it was an outdoor centre.
Alistair:	It is an outdoor centre. Why do you think we're here? We're going to do outdoor activities – sailing, hillwalking, canoeing, orienteering. Remember?
Jamie:	But – the seventeenth century? I thought it was modern – with a swimming pool and a video and a games room.
David:	It is modern. Even a building that dates from the seventeenth century can still have a swimming pool and a video and a games room, silly.
Jamie:	But I thought we were going to modernize it or something.
Alistair:	We're only going to paint the common room and plant some vegetables in the

common room	Aufenthaltsraum
ancient ['eɪnʃənt]	uralt
outdoor centre	Schullandheim
orienteering [ˌɔːrɪənˈtɪərɪŋ]	Orientierungslauf

	garden. And it *has* been modernized since the seventeenth century, MacPhee.
Murdo:	It has got running water and electricity, idiot!
Alistair:	Where have you *been*, MacPhee? You know all this!
Jamie:	I bet it's haunted. Nearly eighty per cent of old houses in Scotland are haunted.
Murdo:	Nonsense. Who told you that?
Jamie:	It's a well-known fact.
Murdo:	Don't be daft.
David:	Who believes in ghosts anyway?
Alistair:	Only babies believe in ghosts.
Jamie:	That's not true. My mother believes in ghosts. And my granny saw a ghost once. She's the seventh child of a seventh child. She's got the second sight.
Alistair:	Sorry, only babies and mothers and grannies believe in ghosts. I certainly don't.
	(The girls arrive.)
Katy:	Typical! 2A boys hide when there's work to be done.
Jamie:	What work? I thought we were going to get our lunch.

the house is haunted ['hɔːntɪd]	es spukt in dem Haus
nonsense ['nɒnsəns]	Quatsch
to have the second sight	hellsehen können

Katy:	We *are* going to get our lunch. But we've to help make it.
	(Everybody groans.)
Morag:	And there's no point in groaning. Everybody has a job.
Jamie:	I'll set the table.
Paula:	Oh no you won't, Jamie MacPhee. Your job is to peel the potatoes.
Jamie:	Who says I have to peel the potatoes? I don't see why I have to peel the potatoes just because you say so.
Paula:	It's not because I say so. Mr Henderson put a list up.
Jamie:	Where is this list?
Katy:	It's on the notice-board in the hall outside the kitchen.
Morag:	She's right.
Katy:	Go and check if you don't believe me! There's a rota. We all take it in turns to do all the different jobs.
Jamie:	I think the girls should do all the cooking and the cleaning and stuff.
Alistair:	Right! And the boys should do all the painting and the gardening.
Jamie:	Yes. Boys are naturally better at that sort of job.

to groan [grəʊn]	stöhnen
to peel	schälen
rota	Dienstplan
to take it in turns to do s. th.	sich bei etwas abwechseln

Morag:	Sexist!
Jamie:	It's not sexist. It's a well-known fact.
Morag:	It's also a well-known fact that Katy got the best grade in 2A for her technical project!
Paula:	Yes, she beat all the boys. So how do you explain that?
	(Anne runs in.)
Anne:	Hey, you lot! Mr Henderson's on the warpath! You should be in the kitchen. Mr Henderson says if lunch is late there will be no trip to the loch this afternoon.

Curtain.

on the warpath	auf dem Kriegspfad
loch [lɒx] *(Scottish)*	der See

Scene Two: The Pudding.

(An hour later in the dining room. The teachers are finishing lunch. 2A and 2B are working in the kitchen.)

Mrs Robertson:	Well, I'm amazed that we've got as far as our pudding after such a bad start.
Mr Henderson:	Indeed! My class had to be late, of course! Typical 2A!
Mrs Robertson:	Then all that mix-up about who does what.
Mr Henderson:	Yes. Where is my list? I put it up on the notice-board myself.
Mrs Robertson:	Well, it's certainly not there now.
Mr Henderson:	And whoever put up this nonsense can hardly write. *(He holds up a paper.)*
Mrs Robertson:	Do you recognise the writing?
Mr Henderson:	No. And I don't think it's funny.
Mrs Robertson:	Look. Poor Jamie MacPhee has to peel all the potatoes and wash all the dishes every day. Well, maybe it's just a wee bit funny!
Mr Henderson:	But not a very clever trick. Even *I* am not quite so unfair!

amazed [əˈmeɪzd]	erstaunt
mix-up	das Durcheinander
wee *(Scottish)*	klein

Mrs Robertson:	But who wants to give poor Jamie such a hard time? Everybody in 2A likes him.
Mr Henderson:	Oh yes. Even if they do think he's a bit eccentric. He's really quite popular. He's their pet professor.
Mrs Robertson:	Maybe somebody in our 2B has a grudge against him.
Mr Henderson:	Maybe it was a mistake to bring 2A and 2B here at the same time. |//
	(A tall figure with a black beard enters, wearing a chef's hat and apron and carrying a large dish.)
Mr Henderson:	Ah, here's the pudding.
Mrs Robertson:	Oh dear, it's rice pudding.
Mr Henderson:	Yes, why is it always rice pudding?
Mrs Robertson:	Ssh, the cook will hear you.
	(The cook puts the dish on the table and disappears through the wall.)
Mrs Robertson:	I thought the pupils were going to serve the meals.
Mr Henderson:	Yes, that's true. It's on the rota.
	(He turns as if to ask the cook.)
	Excuse me, where are the...? Where's he gone?

eccentric [ɪk'sentrɪk]	
their pet professor	ihr Lieblingsprofessor
to have a grudge against s. o.	jemandem böse sein
chef [ʃef]	Chefkoch
cook	Koch
to disappear	verschwinden

Mrs Robertson:	Who?
Mr Henderson:	The cook.
Mrs Robertson:	He's disappeared.
	(Some of class 2A enter.)
Katy:	Mr Henderson, we can't find the pudding.
Morag:	It was on the kitchen table one minute and then ... Oh, there it is.
Mr Henderson:	Yes, the cook brought it in just a moment ago.
Alistair:	But we've just left the cook in the kitchen.
Katy:	He sent us in to tell you we've lost the pudding.
Mr Henderson:	How can you lose the pudding? People don't lose puddings!
Mrs Robertson:	And who was that cook who brought in the pudding?
Mr Henderson:	Yes, a cook definitely brought in the pudding! A big chap with a black beard.
Alistair:	Where is he now?
David:	Where did he disappear to?
Paula:	Well, he didn't go out the window!
Murdo:	And he didn't go out the door!
Alistair:	Because we were coming in!
Murdo:	Exactly!
Mr Henderson:	Very mysterious!

definitely [ˈdefɪnɪtlɪ]   ganz sicher
mysterious [mɪˈstɪərɪəs]   rätselhaft, geheimnisvoll

Mrs Robertson:	Anyway, let's eat the pudding while it's hot. It looks very nice. Ten out of ten!
Anne:	Thank you very much, Mrs Robertson.
Mr Henderson:	Yes, but it's the taste that counts. You know what they say... "The proof of the pudding...
Everybody:	Is in the eating!"

(Mr Henderson takes a spoonful dramatically.)

Mr Henderson:	Aaaaargh! Quick, give me a drink of water!
Mrs Robertson:	What's wrong with it?
Mr Henderson:	It's horrible! It's full of salt. Somebody's put salt in it instead of sugar.
Jamie:	But I put the sugar in, Mr Henderson. Out of a big jar marked "Sugar".
Mr Henderson:	You, Jamie MacPhee! I thought you had to peel potatoes and wash dishes.
Jamie:	That was on the wrong rota, Mr Henderson.
Mr Henderson:	Well, maybe whoever wrote that rota was right. Maybe that's all you're any good at.

(Suddenly the door slams shut, followed by the sound of breaking glass. Loud laughter echoes round the room. Then, after a few moments' silence...)

---

the proof of the pudding...	Probieren geht über Studieren
horrible ['---]	scheußlich

Jamie:	I said the place was haunted.
Katy:	Don't be daft. Somebody's playing a trick on us.
Jamie:	On our class, you mean?
Katy:	Yes, on 2A.
Jamie:	Well, obviously it must be 2B.
Mrs Robertson:	Why, for goodness sake? Look, I'm in charge of 2B and they're perfectly normal, nice pupils. Well, most of them are ... most of the time ... Well, anyway, they're no worse than you. And they don't have anything against you as far as I know.
Jamie:	Oh, I think you'll find I'm right, Mrs Robertson.
Mrs Robertson:	But why are they playing tricks on you?
Jamie:	It's obvious. It's because they know we're going to beat them at everything.
Alistair:	Because we're better at everything.
David:	We're better at canoeing ...
Paula:	And sailing ...
Murdo:	And orienteering.
Jamie:	So they're trying to show that we're no good at cooking. It's as simple as that.

to play a trick on s. o.	jdm. einen Streich spielen
obviously ['ɒbvɪəslɪ]	offensichtlich
for goodness sake!	um Gotteswillen!
to be in charge of s. th.	für etwas die Verantwortung haben

Murdo:	Yes, 2B are just jealous of 2A.
Paula:	Of course they are. We're such a brilliant class.
Jamie:	That's right. It's a well-known fact! *(The teachers groan.)*

Curtain.

jealous [ˈdʒeləs]	neidisch, eifersüchtig
brilliant [ˈbrɪljənt]	hervorragend, hochbegabt

▶

to convince	überzeugen
to spoil	verderben
to scuffle	poltern
to bump into each other	zusammenstoßen

Scene Three: The Highlander.

(Boys' room. Some of class 2B.)

Mrs Robertson:	Goodnight, boys.
All:	Goodnight, Mrs Robertson.
Mrs Robertson:	The girls are already asleep. So I don't want to hear a sound. Is that understood?
All:	Yes, Mrs Robertson.
Mrs Robertson:	You've got a lot to do tomorrow. You've got to beat 2A at orienteering for one thing –
Michael:	And in the table tennis tournament!
Mrs Robertson:	– and for another you've got to convince Mr Henderson that you don't play tricks and spoil food in the kitchen! Is that understood?
All:	Yes, Mrs Robertson.
Mrs Robertson:	Good. Goodnight then, boys.
All:	Goodnight, Mrs Robertson.
	(She puts the lights out, goes out and shuts the door. There's silence for a few seconds).
Michael:	Right. Let's go.
	(There's the sound of scuffling as they bump into each other.)
Robert:	Ouch! Who's that?
Tom:	Who stood on my toe?

Willie:	It's me. Willie MacDuff.
Tom:	Idiot! Who's got the torch?
Willie:	I have.
Robert:	Well, switch it on, Willie.
Willie:	Right.
Robert:	That's better.
Tom:	Come on, let's get the sheets off the beds!
Michael:	Do you think we should go ahead if the girls are asleep?
Willie:	They're probably too frightened. Typical girls.
Tom:	They're not sleeping. They're just pretending in order to get rid of Mrs Robertson.
Robert:	Ssh, I think I can hear them coming. *(Four girls come in carrying sheets.)*
Alison:	OK, let's get organized!
Jim:	Right. We go into 2A girls' room and give them a good fright.
Willie:	Right. They'll be more frightened than the boys.
Joan:	I don't know about that.
Heather:	Boys are just as frightened of ghosts as girls.
Willie:	Girls are always afraid of the dark in any case.

torch [tɔ:tʃ]	Taschenlampe
sheet	Bettlaken
to pretend to do	so tun, als ob
to get rid of s. th.	etwas loswerden

Joan:	Nonsense!
Heather:	What a cheek!
Michael:	Oh, stop arguing. Now, we must be quick, so that we get back to bed before they know who it is.
Lorna:	They'll know it's some of 2B anyway.
Tom:	They think that we ruined their pudding.
Alison:	And they think that we changed the rota.
Joan:	So they're sure to think that we're the ghosts.
Robert:	No they're not. Jamie MacPhee has convinced them that the place is haunted.
Willie:	Maybe it *is* haunted.
Michael:	Oh, don't be silly, Willie!
Willie:	Well, nobody could explain how the window banged shut when there was no wind.
Lorna:	That's true. And there was that funny laugh!
Willie:	And we know that we didn't put the salt in the sugar jar, so who did?
Michael:	Are we going to argue all night or are we going to haunt 2A?
Robert:	OK. Get your sheets on everybody!
Joan:	How many torches have we? I've got one.
Willie:	And me.

what a cheek! so eine Frechheit!
to argue ['ɑ:gju:] streiten

Alison:	Me, too.
Joan:	Good. That's three. Right. Once we're all in their room we count to three, then switch them on suddenly and make a ghosty noise.
Willie:	Like this – wooooooo!
Michael:	Ssh, idiot! You'll wake everybody up before we start. OK. Line up, everybody!
Joan:	Now, switch the torches off just now. And we don't switch them on again till we get into their room. OK?
Michael:	Off we go then! *(The eight 2B ghosts line up one behind the other and move towards the door. At the same time the door opens and in comes another line of ghosts. They bump into each other, fall over their sheets in a heap. Torches go on and off as they are dropped on the floor.)*
Alison:	Ouch, you're going the wrong way, you idiot. The door's that way.
Morag:	I know, silly. I've just come in through the door.
Robert:	Who are you?
Jamie:	Ouch. Someone's standing on my foot!
David:	Who kicked me?
Katy:	Look out! You've torn my sheet.

to wake s. o. up	jemanden wecken
to drop	fallen lassen

Joan:	Where's my torch?
Jamie:	Ouch. Someone's standing on my hand!
Alistair:	Whose foot is this?
Heather:	Who's pulling my hair?
Jamie:	Ouch. Someone's standing on my stomach!
Joan:	Give me back my torch!
Alison:	That's my torch!
Joan:	Let go!
Alison:	Now you've broken it!
Jamie:	Ouch! Someone's standing on my face! *(Suddenly the light goes on. Mrs Robertson and Mr Henderson stand in the doorway and look at the heap of ghosts on the floor.)*
Mr Henderson:	So! It's 2B up to their tricks again, is it? Well, if this continues 2B are going to be on their way home before the week has even started!
Mrs Robertson:	But it's not just 2B this time, Mr Henderson. There are some visitors here from 2A. There's Jamie MacPhee for example.
Mr Henderson:	What are you doing here in the 2B boys' room, Jamie? And Alistair and David and the rest of you?
Alistair:	Well, we had to get our revenge on 2B for the pudding.

to let go	loslassen
heap	Haufen
revenge [rɪˈvendʒ]	Rache

Willie:	We didn't touch your rotten pudding!
Mrs Robertson:	That's quite enough, thank you, Willie MacDuff.
Mr Henderson:	I'm going to count up to ten and if everybody is not back in bed and the lights out I'll want to know why. And above all I want silence. Do you understand? Silence. Absolute silence. If I hear a single sound between now and seven thirty tomorrow morning I'll – *(At that moment there is the unmistakable sound of bagpipes. It seems to be coming from the corridor outside.)*
Mr Henderson:	What nonsense is this now? These practical jokes must stop immediately... *(A huge Highlander playing the bagpipes comes in, marches round the room and out the door again. After a moment's silence everyone rushes after him. The bagpipes stop and there is a loud peal of laughter.)*

Curtain.

rotten	mies
silence ['saıləns]	Ruhe
unmistakable [--'--]	unverkennbar
bagpipes	Dudelsack
a peal of laughter	schallendes Gelächter

Scene Four: The Flag.

(The scene is the common room which is covered in dustsheets as it is being painted by 2B. They all have paint brushes and are painting the walls. They take a drink of coke or coffee from time to time and leave glasses and cups on chairs and on the floor.)

Heather:	Well, I think it must be a ghost.
Alison:	But there's no such thing.
Heather:	Well, who else could it have been?
Michael:	It wasn't one of 2B.
Robert:	And half of 2A were haunting us at the time. And it definitely wasn't a girl.
Tom:	And anyway he was too tall.
Lorna:	I know. It was an adult. It wasn't a pupil at all.
Tom:	And he had a beard and hairy legs.
Lorna:	Yes, it was a long red beard.
Tom:	No, a black beard! Maybe it was a pupil with a false beard.
Joan:	But if he was a pupil, how did he disappear?
Lorna:	And if he was an adult, how did he disappear? He just disappeared into the wall.
Heather:	He was definitely a ghost.
dustsheet	Tuch (z. Abdecken von Möbeln)
beard [bɪəd]	Bart

Alison:	But ghosts don't play the bagpipes.
Heather:	Why not?
Robert:	Yes, how do you know ghosts don't play the bagpipes?
Tom:	There's no rule that says ghosts don't play the bagpipes.
Heather:	And if you don't believe in ghosts, how do you know what they do or don't do?
Michael:	What's more important is that nobody in 2A or 2B plays the bagpipes.
	(There's a pause.)
Alison:	Are you sure about that?
Michael:	Yep!
Heather:	Gosh!
Alison:	Do any of the teachers play the bagpipes?
Michael:	Who knows?
Robert:	But teachers don't play tricks like that.
Joan:	And anyway that still doesn't explain how he disappeared.
Heather:	Into thin air.
Tom:	Into the wall.
Alison:	Maybe there's a secret passage.
Tom:	The wall's not thick enough.
	(At this point Willie MacDuff runs in.)
Michael:	Where have you been?
Alison:	Hiding when there's work to be done as usual.
Willie:	Listen, I know where the Highlander disappeared to last night.

Alison:	Where?
Robert:	How do you know?
Tom:	You were with us.
Lorna:	You didn't see any more than we did.
Willie:	Shut up and let me tell you.
Alison:	Go on then.
Willie:	He climbed up onto the roof.
Michael:	How do you know?
Heather:	And how did he do that while he was playing the bagpipes?
Joan:	And he didn't stop playing the bagpipes all night.
Alison:	I know. Nobody got any sleep.
Michael:	Come on, Willie MacDuff. How can you possibly tell that he climbed up onto the roof?
Willie:	Will you shut up and let me tell you! He left something up there.
Lorna:	What?
Willie:	He left a flag on the flagpole.
Robert:	What sort of flag?
Michael:	And how do you know it was the Highlander who left it?
Willie:	Because it's an ancient flag. It's apparently very very very old. And nobody knows where it came from. And guess what ... It's the MacPhee flag!
Alison:	The MacPhee flag? There's no such thing.

flag   Fahne

Willie:	How do you know? Anyway, it's a flag with the MacPhee clan's coat of arms on it.
Alison:	Well there you are. That proves it wasn't a ghost. It was Jamie MacPhee making a fool of everybody.
Michael:	Oh, really? And how do you explain the fact that at the very moment the Highlander started playing his pipes Jamie MacPhee was lying on the floor of our room tied up in a sheet. And I was sitting on his stomach!
Willie:	There you are! Of course it wasn't Jamie.
Alison:	Anyway, can we believe you, Willie? Is there really a flag on the flagpole?
Robert:	I bet he's just having us on!
Willie:	Well, why don't you come and see it for yourselves?
Robert:	Is it still up on the flagpole?
Willie:	No. Mr Henderson and the warden are examining it in the kitchen. They're quite excited about it. Nobody's ever seen it before. They don't know where it's come from.
Michael:	Right, we're just about finished this wall. Let's go and see the ghost's flag.

coat of arms	Wappen
to make a fool of s. o.	jemanden zum Narren halten
to have s. o. on *(informal)*	jmd. auf den Arm nehmen

Willie:	But give me your coffee cups and coke glasses first, everybody! Mr Henderson told me to bring them back to the kitchen.
	(Willie loads the tray as everybody goes out the door. Willie then walks across to Alison who is waiting at the door with the key in her hand. As Willie gets to the centre of the room he flies forward as if pushed from behind, and tray and contents crash onto the floor, as if knocked from his hand. As he staggers forward he shouts out.)
Willie:	Who did that?
	(There is a loud peal of laughter.)

Curtain.

tray	Tablett
to stagger	taumeln

Scene Five: The Writing on the Wall.

(*The scene is the common room half an hour later. 2A, 2B, Mr Henderson and Mrs Robertson are looking at the newly painted wall. Across it is written in large red letters "Death to the Clan MacDuff".*)

Mr Henderson:	You're absolutely sure you locked the door, Alison?
Alison:	Yes, Mr Henderson. I thought it was safer.
Mr Henderson:	What do you mean, safer?
Alison:	Well, after all the things that have happened.
Jamie:	The ghosts.
Katy:	There's no such thing as ghosts, Jamie.
Mr Henderson:	You mean the practical jokes.
Alison:	Well, really, I just thought somebody could fall over the pots of paint or something. And there was the mess from Willie's accident with the tray.
Willie:	That was no accident! Somebody pushed me!
Mrs Robertson:	It was a bit silly to leave the room with the job half-finished and the paint pots lying about.
Mr Henderson:	Exactly. Somebody obviously got in and painted that on the wall.
Willie:	Death to the Clan MacDuff! What a cheek!

Mr Henderson:	Well, this is the last straw. I think we're all going to have to go back to Edinburgh tomorrow.
Mrs Robertson:	I agree. Just look at the mess. What a waste of paint!
Mr Henderson:	What a waste of money!
Mrs Robertson:	What a waste of time!
Mr Henderson:	If I find out that this was the work of 2A trying to play a stupid trick on 2B ... I'm warning you, you'll go home right away. Your parents will be informed and you will have to pay for the paint that's been wasted.
David:	But, Mr Henderson we wouldn't be so stupid. We'd know that you would suspect us right away.
Alistair:	And, Mr Henderson, if the door was locked how could anyone get in?
Morag:	That's right. Are there any other keys?
Mr Henderson:	Not as far as I know.
Jamie:	See, it's the ghosts again. Maybe it was that big Highlander who put the MacPhee flag up on the flagpole.
Mr Henderson:	Don't be silly, Jamie. There's no such thing as ghosts.
Jamie:	But sir, only a ghost could get in through a locked door.

this is the last straw	jetzt reicht's aber
waste [weɪst]	Verschwendung
to suspect [–ˈ–]	verdächtigen

Mrs Robertson:	It *is* all a bit strange, Jack ... I mean, Mr Henderson.
Mr Henderson:	Oh, come on, don't tell me you believe this nonsense about ghosts now.
Mrs Robertson:	Well, that MacPhee flag is a bit mysterious. And it does look very, very old.
Willie:	And Mr Henderson, what about the Highlander?
Michael:	Lots of people saw him.
Robert:	And how do you explain the fact that somebody got in here through a locked door when the room is on the first floor?
Mr Henderson:	I can't explain it just now. But there is an explanation!
Jamie:	But Mr Henderson, how do you explain the fact that we're painting the wall white, and the paint in the pots is white, and the writing on the wall is in red, and there are no pots of red paint anywhere? *(A pause. The door slams. A blood-curdling scream is heard.)*
Mr Henderson:	Stop screaming, girls!
Katy etc:	We're not screaming!
Mrs Robertson:	Who slammed the door?
Jamie:	Nobody was near the door, Mrs Robertson.

to slam	zuknallen
blood-curdling	grauenerregend

Joan:	And the window's not even open; so there's no draught.
Jamie:	It's the ghost. Doors don't just slam on their own. It's a well-known fact.
Joan:	Oh, Mrs Robertson, I don't like this place. I think I would like to go home.
Alison:	Me too, Mrs Robertson.
Mrs Robertson:	Don't be so silly, girls. Can't you see that Jamie is just teasing you? There's no such thing as ghosts. Mr Henderson is quite right. It's a practical joker.
Mr Henderson:	And he's going home as soon as I get my hands on him. Right, first of all I'm going to have a word with the warden and find out who else has keys to this room. We'll soon get to the bottom of this. *(Mr Henderson goes to the door and turns the handle. It's locked.)*
Mr Henderson:	Oh, this is beyond a joke.
Mrs Robertson:	Right. Who locked the door?
Willie:	Who had the key?
Mr Henderson:	Alison had the key. Where's the key, Alison?
Alison:	It's in my pocket, Mr Henderson ... At least ... it was in my pocket ... Oh, I can't find it, Mr. Henderson ...

there is a draught [drɑːft]	es zieht
to tease	auf den Arm nehmen
to get to the bottom of s. th.	einer Sache a. d. Grund gehen

	(She stutters nervously.)
	It's ... it's not there. Oh, I don't know where it is, Mrs Robertson. It was in my pocket. I'm sure I put it back in my pocket when we came back in. It's not my fault, Mrs Robertson.
Mrs Robertson:	It's all right, Alison. Nobody's blaming you. Calm down.
Mr Henderson:	Empty your pockets, everybody. We must get to the bottom of this.
Jamie:	But Mr Henderson, this is ridiculous. Nobody went near the door. We were with you. You saw us.
Mr Henderson:	I'm no longer sure what I do see and what I don't see, Jamie MacPhee!
Jamie:	Do you believe in ghosts now, Mr Henderson?
Mr Henderson:	Be quiet, Jamie, and empty your pockets! *(They bring all sorts of things out of their pockets. Someone is heard at the door.)*
Warden:	*(Shouts through the keyhole.)* Hello, Mr Henderson. Are you there? It's Mr Grant, the warden, here. There's someone on the phone for you. Could you unlock the door?

to blame s. o.	jemanden beschuldigen
to calm down	sich beruhigen
ridiculous [rɪˈdɪkjʊləs]	lächerlich
warden [ˈwɔːdn]	Herbergsvater

Mr Henderson:	I would if I had the key, Mr Grant.
Mr Grant:	But I gave you the key this morning, Mr Henderson.
Mr Henderson:	It has mysteriously disappeared, Mr Grant. Have you got another key?
Mr Grant:	I'm afraid not, Mr Henderson. That was the only key. But don't worry. I'll phone the joiner in the village. He'll get you out!

Curtain.

joiner [ˈdʒɔɪnə]   Schreiner

Scene Six: Costumes.

(2A and 2B are together in the common room making theatrical costumes.)

Katy:	It's obvious that it's a practical joker.
Joan:	The only thing that's obvious is that we won't be ready for the show unless we forget all this nonsense about ghosts.
Alison:	Who talks about ghosts all the time?
Joan:	Come on! We've got to get these costumes finished.
Alistair:	Relax, Joan! Our farewell show is not till tomorrow night. And Alison, we all know who talks about ghosts all the time. Jamie MacPhee.
Alison:	Right. So who wants to convince us that the place is haunted?
Alistair:	Jamie MacPhee.
Morag:	And whose flag was up on the flagpole?
David:	The MacPhee clan's.
Robert:	When did the MacPhees suddenly get a flag?
Joan:	Robert, your costume won't be ready for tomorrow night! Forget the MacPhee flag!

practical joker	Witzbold
farewell	Abschied

Katy:	Jamie has just invented the MacPhee flag.
Joan:	Och, I give up.
Alistair:	But did he make the flag? He didn't have time.
David:	Besides, the teachers think it's genuine.
Alison:	Maybe he brought the flag with him.
Alistair:	Oh, come off it! I don't believe it.
Michael:	Well, do you believe that the ghost brought it?
Joan:	Willie MacDuff said the Highlander put the flag up on the flagpole.
Morag:	And Willie MacDuff said that the Highlander was a ghost.
Alistair:	Well, if you believe Willie MacDuff you'll believe anything.
Katy:	Where is Willie MacDuff, by the way?
Alison:	Avoiding work, as usual.
Lorna:	And where's Jamie MacPhee?
Murdo:	Perhaps they're both playing tricks on us.
David:	Well somebody played a trick on Jamie first of all.
Joan:	When?
David:	When they changed the rota on the day we arrived.

to invent [–'–]	erfinden
genuine ['dʒenjʊɪn]	echt
come off it! *(informal)*	nun mach' mal halblang!
to avoid	vermeiden

Alistair:	That's right! Jamie was going to have to do all the rotten jobs.
Katy:	Then somebody put salt in the jar marked sugar –
Morag:	That's right! And it was Jamie who put the sugar into the pudding.
David:	Somebody was trying to get him into trouble.
Alistair:	Right!
Robert:	Then there was the Highlander.
Michael:	Well, that wasn't Jamie!
Robert:	Yes, we know, Michael. You were sitting on his stomach at the time.
Joan:	But maybe Jamie put the flag on the flagpole.
Alison:	Do you think it was Jamie who painted "Death to the Clan MacDuff" on the wall?
Joan:	Maybe.
Alistair:	But how did Jamie get up onto the roof or into a locked room with no key?
Katy:	So you think that there is a ghost then?
Alistair:	Well ...
Alison:	*(almost in tears)* I wish you'd stop talking about ghosts. Everybody knows there's no such thing as ghosts!
Alistair:	All right, Alison. Calm down. You're ab-

almost in tears   dem Weinen nahe

	solutely right. There's no such thing as ghosts. Isn't she right, everybody? All together after me – THERE'S NO SUCH THING AS GHOSTS!
All:	THERE'S NO SUCH THING AS GHOSTS!
	(Suddenly the lights go out. Everybody screams and shouts. Then there's the sound of bagpipes. The lights go on to reveal a big Highlander playing the bagpipes. He walks slowly across the room.)
Tom:	I told you it was a black beard.
Lorna:	Well, the one I saw had a red beard.
Heather:	I told you he was about seven feet tall!
Alistair:	Come on, everybody! Let's catch him this time!
	(Some of them start to move towards the Highlander.)
Michael:	Wait a minute. *(They all stop.)* There's something funny about this ghost. He seems a bit wobbly...
Robert:	And those aren't real bagpipes! It's a tartan scarf and some wooden spoons!
Morag:	And that's not a kilt! It's a tartan travelling rug!

wobbly	wackelig
tartan	Schottenstoff, Schottenkaro
kilt	Schottenrock
rug	Wolldecke

Katy:	And that sounds like a whole pipe band! It's a cassette!
	(At this point the "Highlander" collapses on the floor.)
Katy:	And that's Jamie MacPhee and Willie MacDuff!
Alison:	Well, I knew all the time that it wasn't a ghost.
Alistair:	Yes, we know, Alison. You've made your point. There's no such thing as ghosts.
Jamie:	Oh, yes there is!
Willie:	He's right. In fact, there's probably two.
Alistair:	Yes, and we've caught them in the act!
Morag:	Now we know who to blame for the salt in the pudding and the writing on the wall.
Robert:	And everything else. We knew it was you two all the time.
Katy:	Stupid idiots! They nearly sent us all home because of your tricks. It was you all the time, wasn't it?
Jamie:	But it wasn't! This is the first time we've done anything. Honestly! Isn't that right, Willie?
Willie:	Of course it is. We couldn't have done the other things. And look how quickly you saw that it wasn't a ghost today!

to catch s. o. in the act	jmd. auf frischer Tat ertappen
honestly	ehrlich

Jamie:	We've found a book in the library which more or less proves that there are ghosts.
Willie:	It's a history of this house.
Alison:	We're not interested in whatever stupid book you've found.
Joan:	Or your flag.
Morag:	Or your ugly big Highlander.
Jamie:	But this book says that MacPhees and MacDuffs lived in this house away back in the eighteenth century.
Willie:	That's right. In fact they were always fighting over it.
Jamie:	So you see it's quite likely that they're still fighting.
Alison:	Don't listen to them. Let's finish these costumes. Go away, Jamie! And you, Willie! We've wasted enough time because of you!
Willie:	But don't you see? It's obvious. The MacPhees and the MacDuffs are angry because we're here. We're in their house.
Katy:	Oh no! Shut up for goodness sake! We're fed up with MacPhees and MacDuffs!
Jamie:	But Willie's right. The MacPhees are angry with him and the MacDuffs are angry with me. It's obvious.

library [ˈlaɪbrərɪ]   Bibliothek
to fight [faɪt], **fought, fought**   kämpfen, streiten
to be fed up with s. th.   etwas satt haben

(Jamie and Willie are standing in the middle of the room with the others on either side of them.)

Jamie: You see, it's like this. The ghosts probably think . . .

Alison: I'm going to scream in a minute! When will you believe me that there's no such thing as ghosts?

Alistair: Come on everybody! Let's show them that there's no such thing as ghosts!

(They all start to shout and scream and jump on Willie and Jamie as the curtain falls.)

Scene Seven: The Lady.

(The common room. It is Saturday evening, just before the farewell show. At one side pupils are busy arranging scenery, watched by the teachers. Another group, including Jamie and Willie, are arranging chairs for the audience.)

Mr Henderson:	Well, I must say there were times when I didn't think we'd get to Saturday evening.
Mrs Robertson:	I agree. It has been a very interesting week!
Warden:	I certainly can't remember a more interesting one!
Mr Henderson:	Well, I hope you think that the old house is now looking a bit better, Mr Grant.
Warden:	Oh, yes, I do indeed. The boys and girls made a lovely job of the common room.
Mrs Robertson:	Eventually!
Alison:	2B are really good at painting, aren't they, Mrs Robertson?
Mrs Robertson:	Let's not talk about that subject, Alison!
Alistair:	And we did some good work in the garden, Mr Henderson.

scenery [ˈsiːnərɪ]   Kulissen, Bühnendekoration
audience [ˈɔːdɪəns]   die Zuschauer
eventually [ɪˈventʃʊəlɪ]   schließlich, am Ende

Mr Henderson:	Yes, I expected some disaster to hit the garden but everything was fine.
Alistair:	And 2A are the best cooks, aren't they, Mrs Robertson?
Mrs Robertson:	Well I don't know if Mr Henderson agrees, Alistair. I seem to remember a certain dish of rice ...
Mr Henderson:	Well, if we get this show over without any disaster I think we can say that the week was a success.
Katy:	Well, we'll soon see who has the funniest sketches in the show!
Morag, David and Alistair:	2A!
Alison, Tom and Michael:	2B!
Mrs Robertson:	For goodness sake, why is everything a competition? Why can't you agree that you'll both put on a good show?
Mr Henderson:	I think we can say that the two classes are equal. 2A won the sailing this afternoon, and 2B won the orienteering yesterday. Excellent! And there were no problems and no disasters.
Alistair:	*(aside)* And no ghosts!

disaster [-'--] Katastrophe
success [sək'ses] Erfolg
excellent ['eksələnt] hervorragend

Mr Henderson:	Well, it's about time for the show to begin, don't you think, Mrs –
	(At this point the lights go out. They hear bagpipes. People scream and shout. The lights go on again. The scenery has been knocked over and everything is in a mess. A big Highlander is marching up and down playing the pipes.)
Alison:	Oh no! Not those two idiots again! Jamie MacPhee and Willie MacDuff. They're up to their tricks again.
	(She runs towards the Highlander.)
Mr Henderson:	Well, that's it! The show's cancelled!
Jamie and Willie:	But, Mr Henderson, we've done nothing! We're over here.
Mrs Robertson:	It's not Jamie and Willie this time.
Alison:	*(Doesn't see Jamie and Willie.)*
	Oh, yes it is! Let's teach them another lesson, everybody. There's no such thing as ghosts!
	(She is about to jump on the piper when the chandelier crashes down, just missing the piper and Alison. At the same time a second Highlander comes in from

to cancel [ˈkænsl]	absagen
to teach s. o. a lesson	jemandem eine Lektion erteilen
chandelier [ˌʃændəˈlɪə]	Kronleuchter

	the left playing a different tune. The two pipers face each other and continue to play. Jamie shouts to Willie.)
Jamie:	See, I was right. There are two of them. I told you!
Willie:	I told you, you mean. I knew they were playing tricks on each other.
Voice:	Yes, they have been playing tricks on each other and it's got to stop this minute!
	(The pipers stop playing and bow their heads like scolded children. A lady appears and stands between them. She is wearing a long white dress and a tartan sash.)
Lady:	You've been fighting for two centuries, and it's got to stop now!
	(The two pipers mutter at each other.)
Lady:	That's enough from you, *(sarcastic)* Red Hector of the Battles. Look at what you've done! I'm ashamed to call you my husband. Start clearing up this mess!

tune [tju:n]	Melodie
to scold	ausschimpfen
sash	Schärpe
to mutter	murren
battle	Schlacht
Red Hector of the Battles	Der Name eines historischen Clanoberhauptes mit roten Haaren
to be ashamed	sich schämen

(Hector puts down his pipes and starts picking up chairs.)

Lady: And as for you, Black Angus MacDuff, my good-for-nothing brother! How many times must I tell you that it's *my* business who I marry – even if it is a MacPhee! Clear up that chandelier. You nearly killed that poor wee girl. That's it finished. NOW!!!

(The two pipers pause for a moment to groan, raise their eyes to heaven, shake their heads and mutter.)

Lady: Come on, boys! No nonsense!

(She winks at the others.)

Lady: That's the spirit!

(She claps her hands and the lights go out again. Everyone starts to shout or laugh or scream. The sound of the pipes is heard in the distance. The lights go on again and everything is in order. The chandelier is back in place. The lady and the two Highlanders have gone.)

Mr Henderson: Was that part of the concert or am I going crazy?

good-for-nothing	nichtsnutzig
it's my business	es geht nur mich an
to wink	blinzeln, zwinkern
that's the spirit!	so ist's recht!
to go crazy	verrückt werden

Katy:	Well, it certainly wasn't part of the concert!
Mr Henderson:	Then I must be going crazy!
Alison:	*(doubtfully)* There is no such thing as ghosts. Isn't that right, Mrs Robertson?
Jamie:	Oh yes, there is! It's a well-known fact. And my great, great, great, great, great granny has just proved it!

Curtain.

---

doubtfully [ˈdaʊtfʊlɪ]   unsicher, voller Zweifel
great ... granny   Ur ... großmutter

Teacher's Notes

The play is set in the Scottish Highlands, a part of Scotland which until the late eighteenth century was divided into clan lands. The language spoken was Gaelic. *Clan* means children or family, *Mac* means son. Thus Clan Donald means the descendants of Donald, MacDonald being the clan members' surname. The clans fought one another frequently, and were often caught up in wider political conflicts. These rivalries led to feuds, the most famous of which is that between MacDonalds and Campbells. Campbell means "twisted mouth". Not all clan names begin with Mac – some, like Clan Campbell, adopted a descriptive nickname.

The main characters are: two teachers, three ghosts, Jamie and Willie; Alison, Katy, Alistair and Joan. There are speaking and non-speaking parts for as many others as circumstances dictate. Some "crowd scenes" are included. In others a number of characters engage in excited discussion, in which they almost, but not quite, speak at the same time or interrupt one another.

The supernatural scenes present a challenge to the ingenuity of the director(s) – characters walk through walls, props crash to the ground and break, only to be reinstated under cover of darkness. With imaginative use of curtains and lighting this should not present an insurmountable problem. The pupils who do not wish to be on stage could be put in charge of the technical side of the production so that the whole class is involved actively in the play.